•大喜說故事系列•

Tashi

and the
FORTUNE TELLER

大喜與算命仙

Anna Fienberg
Barbara Fienberg 著

Kim Gamble 繪

王盟雄 譯

三民書局

'**F**unny how **crocodile** tastes almost exactly like chicken,' remarked Dad.

'Yes, same **chewy** white meat,' said Mom.

Uncle Joe **stared** very hard at his plate.

'Actually,' he said, after a long pause, 'they were out of crocodile at the supermarket. Fancy! In Tiabulo, where I've just come from, you can buy it everywhere: canned, baked, boiled...Great for late night suppers when the fish aren't jumping.'

老爸說，「真奇怪，鱷魚肉吃起來怎麼跟雞肉差不多。」

老媽說，「對呀，一樣都是耐嚼的白肉。」

喬大叔兩眼直盯著他的盤子。「事實上，」他停頓了好一會兒才又繼續說，「超級市場裡的鱷魚肉已經賣完了。真搞不懂！我才剛從提耳布洛來，那裡到處都買得到鱷魚肉：罐裝的、火烤的、水煮的……當深夜捕不到魚的時候，拿來當晚餐吃實在太棒了。」

crocodile [`krɑkə͵daɪl] 名 鱷魚
chewy [`tʃuɪ] 形 有嚼勁的
stare [stɛr] 動 瞪視

'Thank the stars we don't live in Tiabulo,' Dad whispered to Jack, behind his hand.

It was Sunday, and the family were sitting down to lunch. It was a late lunch because Uncle Joe had taken ages to cook it, but Tashi had only just arrived. He'd been making the **dessert**.

'Have you ever tried **ghost** pie?' asked Tashi.

'It's a secret **recipe** learned from ghosts I once knew.'

'No,' said Uncle Joe, 'but I remember a fortune teller once said —'

'Luk Ahed?' asked Jack.

'No, another one, in the Carribean Islands. Anyway, this man told me that when I was forty-three I would visit my brother and meet a wise young lad who would **offer** me a most mysterious dessert.'

老爸用手掩著嘴巴小聲地對傑克說，「謝天謝地，我們不住在提耳布洛。」

今天是星期天，全家人都坐下來一起吃午餐。因為喬大叔煮了老半天，午餐很晚才開動。不過大喜因為之前忙著做甜點，所以現在才剛到而已。

「你們吃過鬼派嗎？」大喜問。「它的祕方是從我以前認識的鬼那裡學來的。」

「沒有，」喬大叔說，「但是我記得有個算命仙曾經說過——」

「是盧半仙嗎？」傑克問。

「不是，是另外一個，住在加勒比海群島。總之，這個人告訴我，當我四十三歲的時候，我會來拜訪我哥哥，而且會遇見一位聰明的少年，他會給我一種最不可思議的點心。」

dessert [dɪˋzɝt] 名 甜點
ghost [gost] 名 鬼
recipe [ˋrɛsəpɪ] 名 烹調法
offer [ˋɔfɚ] 動 提供

'Aha!' Dad smacked his forehead. 'Ghost pie! Eat a slice and walk through walls. What's more mysterious than that? Your fortune **came true** then, didn't it?'

'Sometimes it does,' Tashi said slowly, 'and sometimes it doesn't.'

Jack looked hard at Tashi. 'Did you go back and see *your* fortune teller?'

Tashi nodded. 'Yes, and it wasn't long before I wished I'd never stepped foot in the place.' He put his fork down. 'Luk Ahed had been so **clever** telling me about the magic shoes, I decided to visit him again. I thought maybe he'd find some more surprises in my **horoscope**.'

'And *did* he?' asked Dad eagerly.

'You can *bet* on it,' said Uncle Joe, playing hard with his peas. 'They always do.'

「哇塞！」老爸拍了一下額頭。「鬼派！吃個一片就能穿牆而過。還有什麼比那更不可思議的？這個預言應驗了，不是嗎？」

「有時候預言會應驗，」大喜緩緩地說，「有時候則不會。」

傑克的眼光緊緊盯著大喜。「你有回去找過算命仙嗎？」

大喜點點頭。「有。但是不久之後，我就希望沒有去過那個地方。」他放下叉子。「盧半仙曾經告訴我關於寶鞋的事，而它也真的應驗了，所以我決定再去找他。我想或許他可以從我的命盤裡看出更多令人吃驚的事。」

「結果有算出來嗎？」老爸急切地追問。

「當然，」喬大叔冒出一句，一邊很認真地撥弄著盤裡的豌豆。「那些算命仙總是鐵口直斷。」

come true 實現

clever [`klɛvɚ] 形 聰明的

horoscope [`hɔrəˌskop] 名 天宮圖

'More than I'd ever **bargained** for,' agreed Tashi. 'See, it was like this. Luk Ahed was just finishing his breakfast when I arrived, but he put down his pancake and licked his fingers. He was like that—always happy to see you, always eager to help. It was only a few days since my last visit to him, so my chart hadn't been completely **buried** under his books and papers.

'"Here it is!" he cried, pulling it out. He was so surprised and pleased with himself at finding it quickly that he did a little jig and almost upset his breakfast over the table. "Come and sit beside me on the bench while I read, Tashi," he invited.

「事情的確出乎我意料之外，」大喜同意。「這個嘛，事情是這樣的。我到的時候盧半仙已經快吃完早餐了，但他一看到我就放下煎餅，舔了舔手指頭。他向來這樣——總是笑臉迎人、總是熱心幫忙。因為幾天前我才找過他，所以我的命盤還沒完全淹沒在他的書和紙堆裡。

　　「『找到了！』他喊著，將它抽了出來。能這麼快找到東西讓他又驚又喜，他興奮地蹦跳了一下，卻差一點打翻桌子上的早餐。『大喜，過來坐在我旁邊的凳子上，我講給你聽。』他邀請著。

bargain [`bɑrgən] 勔 期待《for》
bury [`bɛrɪ] 勔 埋藏

'"Anyone who has already had such an exciting life as yours would be sure to have a very interesting future ahead of him."

'Well, I watched him read for a minute, and then suddenly he stopped smiling and covered his eyes with his hands.

'"Oh, Tashi," he said in a **sorrowful** voice.

'"What? What is it?"

'"Oh, Tashi, on the morning of your 10th birthday you are going to **die**!"

'"But that will be the day after tomorrow! Are you sure, Luk Ahed? I'm so **healthy** — look!" I jumped up and down and did one-arm push ups to show him I wasn't even **breathing** hard.

「『任何人經歷過像你這樣刺激的生活以後，一定會有個很有趣的未來。』

「於是，我就看著他算了一分鐘，但突然間他的笑容不見了，還用手遮住雙眼。

「『喔！大喜！』他用一種悲哀的口氣說。

「『怎麼樣？是怎麼一回事？』

「『喔！大喜，在你十歲生日的那天早上，你就會死去！』

「『可是那就是後天呀！盧半仙，你有沒有搞錯？我這麼健康——你看！』我跳上跳下，還做了單手伏地挺身，讓他知道我能臉不紅、氣不喘地做這些事。

sorrowful [ˋsɑrofəl] 形 悲傷的

die [daɪ] 動 死掉

healthy [ˋhɛlθɪ] 形 健康的

breathe [brɪð] 動 呼吸

11

'Luk Ahed shook his head sadly. "I'm sorry, Tashi, but we can't **argue** with **destiny**."

"'There must be something we can do. Couldn't *you* put in a good word for me?"

'Luk Ahed laughed unhappily. "*I'm* not important enough for that, Tashi. No, once your name has been written in the Great Book of Fate, there is nothing..." He paused. "Except your name hasn't been entered in the Book yet, has it? And it won't be written in until New Year's Eve...in two days' time. And if on that evening you were to..."

'I was beginning to notice that Luk Ahed had a very **annoying** habit of not **finishing** his sentences. "If I were to *what*, Luk Ahed?"

「盧半仙悲傷地搖搖頭。『大喜，我很遺憾，但我們無法跟命運對抗啊！』

「『一定會有辦法的。你難道不能為我消災解厄嗎?』

「盧半仙笑得很勉強。『大喜，我沒有那種本領。沒有用的，一旦你的名字被寫入天書，就沒辦法……』他的聲音忽然停住了。『除非你的名字還沒被寫進天書，對吧?天書都是除夕夜才寫的……還有兩天。假如那天晚上，你……』

「我發現盧半仙有個很討厭的習慣，就是話總是只說到一半。『盧半仙，假如我怎麼樣呢?』

argue [`ɑrgju] 動 爭論
destiny [`dɛstənɪ] 名 命運
annoying [ə`nɔɪɪŋ] 形 惱人的
finish [`fɪnɪʃ] 動 結束

'The fortune teller was feverishly looking through his sacred books. "The Gods like to enjoy a particular meal on New Year's Eve," he said. "Very simple, but **special**. Each God has his own **favorite** dishes. Now, if we were to serve our God of Long Life his own personal special meal, cooked to perfection..."

'"He might put me back in the Book of Life!" I finished his sentence.

'"Exactly."'

'So what are the special dishes?' asked Uncle Joe. 'Not crocodile, by any chance? Braised perhaps, with noodles?'

'No,' Tashi shook his head. 'Wild mushroom omelet with **nightingale** eggs. Speckled **trout** with wine and ginger. And a bowl of golden **raspberries**.'

「算命仙急切地查閱著他的寶典。『神明們喜歡在除夕夜吃大餐，』他說。『很簡單，但必須很特別。每一位神明都有自己喜歡吃的菜。假如我們用長壽之神最喜歡的菜來祭拜他，並且煮得恰到好處……』

「『他就有可能再把我的名字寫進命書！』我替他把話說完。

「『沒錯。』」

「那麼，是哪些特別的菜呢？」喬大叔問。「該不會剛好就是鱷魚肉吧？說不定要和麵一起燉呢？」

「不是，」大喜搖搖頭。「是野生蘑菇蛋捲加上夜鶯蛋、用酒和薑絲調味的斑紋鱒魚、還有一碗黃金覆盆子。」

special [`spɛʃəl] 形 特別的
favorite [`fevərɪt] 形 喜愛的
nightingale [`naɪtɪŋgel] 名 夜鶯
trout [traʊt] 名 鱒魚
raspberry [`ræz,bɛrɪ] 名 覆盆子

'Gosh!' said Dad. 'Where would you get a nightingale egg? *Are* there any in your part of the world, Tashi?'

'Not that I knew of—I'd never seen any **nests** in our forests. For a moment I did feel low, I can tell you. It all seemed impossible. But then I thought of my friend, the **raven**. He *had* said, "Just **whistle** if you ever need my help." Remember when he was hurt after that terrible storm, Jack? The night Baba Yaga blew in? And I knew the children I had rescued from the war lord would gladly **gather** the mushrooms for me. And Lotus Blossom's mother had a **pond** at the bottom of her house where I was almost *sure* I'd seen speckled trout swimming. Maybe it wasn't impossible after all.

「老天！」老爸說。「你到哪裡去找夜鶯蛋？大喜，你們那裡有嗎？」

　　「就我所知道是沒有的——我從來沒有在我們的森林裡看見過鳥巢。老實說，在那時候我的確難過了一下下。這似乎是件不可能做到的事。不過後來我想到我的朋友大烏鴉。他曾經說過，『有事需要我幫忙的話，只要吹口哨就行了。』傑克，還記得他在那次狂風暴雨中受傷了嗎？就是巴巴鴉加被風吹來的那天晚上？而且我知道，我從督軍手上救出來的那些孩子會很樂意幫我採蘑菇的。而阿蓮的媽媽家底下有個池塘，我敢說我曾經看過裡面有斑紋鱒魚。或許要完成這件事並不是不可能。

nest [nɛst] 名 鳥巢

raven [`revn̩] 名 大烏鴉

whistle [`wɪsl̩] 動 吹口哨

gather [`gæðɚ] 動 採集

pond [pɑnd] 名 池塘

'So I hastily said goodbye to Luk Ahed and ran home to the mulberry tree where the raven sometimes **perched**. He flew down at my second whistle and when I told him about the dinner and the nightingale eggs, he said, "Give me your straw basket and I will be back with them tomorrow."

'The village children were very excited when I **explained** about the mushrooms. '"We'll find enough for twenty Gods, Tashi," they shouted. Off they ran with their bags, **clattering** over the bridge into the fields and forest.

「因此我匆匆忙忙地跟盧半仙道別，然後跑到大鳥鴉有時會棲息的那棵桑樹下。才吹了兩聲口哨，他就飛下來了。我告訴他關於那頓大餐和夜鶯蛋的事，他說，『把你的草籃給我，明天我就會把它們帶回來。』

　　「當我跟村裡的孩子們解釋蘑菇的事情時，他們都很興奮。他們大聲地說，『大喜，我們會找到足夠二十位神明吃的蘑菇的。』他們拿著袋子跑掉，嘻嘻哈哈地穿過橋樑、經過原野、進入了森林。

perch [pɝtʃ] 動 棲息

explain [ɪk`splen] 動 解釋

clatter [`klætɚ] 動 喋喋不休

'Meanwhile, I hurried to Lotus Blossom's house. Her mother wasn't so happy to lose the beautiful speckled trout — they were her last three — but she gave a good-hearted smile as she **scooped** them out of her pond and handed them to me in a bowl of water.

'I raced back to the square where Luk Ahed stood, waving his hands. There was a great **argument** going on in the village about who would be the best people to cook the dishes. No one was listening to Luk Ahed, who was calling for order. Finally everyone agreed that Sixth Aunt Chow made the most **delicious** omelets, but that Big Wu and his Younger Brother, Little Wu, should cook the fish.

「同時，我又跑到阿蓮她家。她媽媽並不想要失去這些美麗的斑紋鱒魚——因為只剩下最後三條——但是她還是親切地笑一笑，把魚從池塘裡撈上來，裝進一盆水裡交給我。

「我跑回廣場，盧半仙就站在那裡對我揮手。村子裡已經為了誰是煮菜的最佳人選吵得不可開交。盧半仙要求大家守秩序，可是沒有人理他。最後大家同意，讓周六嬸來做最可口的蛋捲，然後由大吳和他弟弟小吳來煮魚。

scoop [skup] 動 舀起
argument [`ɑrgjəmənt] 名 爭論
delicious [dɪ`lɪʃəs] 形 美味的

'Next morning, cooking fires were set up in the square so everyone could watch and advise. The children were back before noon with beautiful baskets overflowing with four different kinds of mushrooms. In the early afternoon the raven returned. He looked quite **bedraggled** and tired, but in the basket were a dozen perfect nightingale eggs.

'Mrs Li brought out a bottle of her prized wine to add to the fish and I left them all busily chopping ginger roots and celery and bamboo shoots.

'Now the hardest task lay ahead. In all our province I had only ever seen one bush of golden raspberries. And it **belonged** to my enemy, the wicked Baron.'

'Oh, no!' cried Jack.

「第二天早上，廣場上生起煮菜的火來，這樣大家就可以觀看並且提供建議。正午前，孩子們就帶著漂亮的籃子回來了，裡頭裝滿了四種不同的蘑菇。剛過中午不久，大烏鴉也回來了，一副溼淋淋髒兮兮而且疲憊不堪的樣子，可是籃子裡已經有一打完好的夜鶯蛋。

「李太太拿出一瓶得過獎的酒倒在魚上，我則放手讓他們忙著切薑絲、芹菜、和竹筍。

「現在最棘手的任務來了。全省裡頭，我只看過一株黃金覆盆子。偏偏那株覆盆子又是我的敵人，就是那個壞地主所有。」

傑克喊，「哦，不會吧！」

bedraggled [bɪˋdrægəld] 形 髒兮兮的
belong [bɪˋlɔŋ] 動 屬於

'Oh, yes!' said Tashi. 'I had brought my magic shoes with me but I decided not to put them on. As I walked slowly to his house I went over in my mind exactly *how* I would go about asking the Baron for a bowl of his berries.

'But I didn't have to ask. He had already heard the news and he was waiting for me with a fat smile on his face.

'"Well, Tashi," he **gloated**, "I hear that you are in need of some of my berries."

'"Yes, please."

「沒錯，就是這樣！」大喜說。「我隨身帶著寶鞋，可是還是決定不要穿上它。當我慢慢走向他家時，心裡一直在想，要怎樣開口跟壞地主要一碗覆盆子。

　　「可是我用不著問，他就已經知道這個消息，擺出大大的笑臉等著我了。

　　「『唷，大喜，』他幸災樂禍地對我說，『聽說你很需要我的覆盆子。』

　　「『是的，請給我一些吧！』

gloat [glot] 動 興災樂禍地說

'"Oh, you'll have to do much better than that." He shook a playful finger at me. "Something like this. Now, Tashi, say after me: Please, please most kindly, honorable and worthy Baron, could you give some berries to this miserable little worm Tashi, who stands before you?"

'I **gritted** my teeth and managed to force out the words, but the Baron **pretended** he couldn't hear and made me say it all over again. When I had finished, he **thumped** his fist on the table and shouted, "No, I couldn't! After all the trouble you have caused me, I'll be glad to **be rid of** you. Not a berry will you have."

「『噢，這樣太便宜你了。』他開玩笑似地搖搖手指頭。『這樣吧！來，大喜，跟著我說：拜託，最仁慈、最尊貴、最了不起的大地主，求求你把覆盆子賜給站在你面前的可憐蟲大喜，好嗎？』

「我咬緊牙關，努力把那些話從嘴裡擠出來，不料壞地主卻假裝聽不見，要我重頭再說一遍。說完以後，他卻碰地一聲用拳頭重重地敲了一下桌子，大喊，『不要，我不給你！在你給我惹了這麼多麻煩以後，我巴不得能擺脫掉你。連一顆覆盆子你也別想得到。』

grit [grɪt] 動 咬緊牙關
pretend [prɪˋtɛnd] 動 假裝
thump [θʌmp] 動 重擊
be rid of 擺脫

27

'I was just leaving his house when Third Aunt called after me. She worked in the Baron's kitchen, remember, Jack? Well, she came close and whispered, "There *is* another bush of golden raspberries, Tashi. It belongs to the Old **Witch** who lives in the forest. But don't take any without asking her. The berries **scream** if anyone except the witch picks them."

'Oh dear, I didn't like the sound of that but what was I to do? It was the Old Witch's berries or none.

'This time I slipped my magic shoes on and I was in the forest in a few bounds. I found the witch's cottage and there in the garden at the back of the house was a small raspberry bush. There were only a few golden berries on it but they looked round and juicy. I **touched** one gently and it gave a little scream.

「正當我要離開他家的時候，三嬸在背後叫住我。傑克，還記得她在壞地主的廚房工作吧？她走了過來，低聲說，『大喜，還有一個地方也有長覆盆子，是住在森林裡的老巫婆的。但是可別沒問過她就先拿。除了巫婆本人以外，任何人去摘，那些覆盆子都會發出尖叫聲。』

　　「哦，天啊，我不喜歡那種聲音，可是該怎麼辦呢？除了跟老巫婆求救以外，已經沒有其他的辦法了。

　　「這次我把寶鞋穿上，才跳了幾下，就來到了森林裡。我找到巫婆的小屋，屋子後面的花園裡有一小叢覆盆子，上面只長了幾顆黃金覆盆子，但它們看起來飽滿又多汁。我輕輕地碰了一顆，它果然叫了一聲。

witch [wɪtʃ] 名 巫婆
scream [skrim] 動 尖叫
touch [tʌtʃ] 動 觸碰

'A door opened at once and a **bony** old figure
in a dusty black cloak came hobbling down the
path.

'"Who is **meddling** with my raspberry bush?"
she shrieked.

「接著，門立刻就開了。一個瘦得只剩皮包骨的老太婆，穿著一件滿是灰塵的黑披風，腳一跛一跛地從小徑走來。

「『是誰在亂碰我那叢覆盆子？』她尖聲喊。

bony [`bonɪ] 形 骨瘦如材的
meddle [`mɛdl̩] 動 摸弄《with》

'She looked like a bunch of old broom sticks strung together. She was even more **hideous** than people had said. Her blackened teeth were bared in a fierce growl and her bristly chin was **thrust** out so far in rage that her beak almost touched it. I turned to run. I expected my magic shoes would take me to safety in one bound, but something in the way she stood there, alone on the garden path, made me stop. Her mouth **puckered** around her gums and her eyes were sad. Come to think of it, I had never heard of her **harming** anyone.

'I took a deep breath and said, "I was just looking at them, Granny, because I have a great need of golden raspberries at the moment."

「她那副樣子就好像是幾根舊掃把綑在一起似的，比傳聞中恐怖多了。她張嘴一吼，露出她那一口黑黑的牙齒；一生氣發起火來，那長滿硬毛的下巴就外凸得很厲害，簡直就快碰到她的鷹鉤鼻了。我轉身準備逃跑，希望縱身一跳，寶鞋就會把我帶到安全的地方。可是她獨自站在花園小徑上的神態，讓我不由自主地停下腳步。她的嘴乾乾癟癟的，眼神中透露出一種悲傷。仔細想想，其實我從來也沒聽說她有害過誰。

　　「我深深吸了一口氣說，『奶奶，我只是看看它們而已，因為我現在非常需要黃金覆盆子。』」

hideous [`hɪdɪəs] 形 可怕的
thrust [θrʌst] 動 伸出
pucker [`pʌkə] 動 皺起
harm [hɑrm] 動 傷害

'She **cackled**. "Oh, you have, have you?" And she sat herself down on a bench. "Tell me about it then."

'When I had finished, she pulled herself up on my arm. She grinned at me, and with her mouth no longer set in a growl and her eyes **sparkling** with interest, she didn't look nearly so scary. "Come on then," she said, "we'll make a nice pot of tea and then you can pick your berries. There aren't many left but you'll find enough to fill a bowl, I'm sure."

「她哈哈大笑。『噢，你需要，是嗎？』然後她坐在長凳上。『告訴我為什麼。』

　　「我說完以後，她扶著我的手站起來，對我咧嘴微笑，嘴巴不再因咆哮而張大，眼中流露出感興趣的光芒，看起來也沒那麼可怕了。『來吧，』她說，『讓我們先泡壺茶，你再去摘覆盆子。覆盆子已經剩下不多了，不過我敢保證還夠裝滿一碗。』

cackle [`kækl̩] 勔 呵呵笑
sparkle [`spɑrkl̩] 勔 閃閃發亮

'You can imagine how joyfully I ran back with my basket of fruit. But when I reached the bridge by the Baron's house, he was standing there, **blocking** my way. His eyes bulged when he saw my berries and with a roar of rage he **charged** towards me and **knocked** the basket up in the air and into the river. I hung over the railing and watched in despair as the berries bobbed away **downstream**.

'"How are you going to prepare your wonderful meal now, eh, clever Tashi?" the Baron sneered.

「你可以想像當我帶著裝滿覆盆子的籃子跑回來的時候，心裡有多麼高興。可是到了壞地主家旁邊的那座小橋時，他就站在那裡，擋住了我的去路。當他看見我的覆盆子時，立刻瞪大了眼睛，生氣地大吼一聲朝我撲了過來，把籃子撞到半空中，然後掉進河裡。我靠在欄杆上，絕望地看著覆盆子隨著河水漂到下游去。

「『我說，聰明的大喜啊，你現在要怎麼準備你那頓大餐啊？』壞地主冷冷地笑著。

block [blɑk] 動 擋住
charge [tʃɑrdʒ] 動 衝向
knock [nɑk] 動 撞倒
downstream [ˌdaun`strim] 副 順流地

'I struggled to hold in my bitter feelings and faced him calmly. "We'll prepare the rest of the meal and I will take it to the mountain top, to the *Gods*, together with a **note** explaining that the delicious golden raspberries are missing because the wicked Baron, *YOU*, knocked them into the river."

'The Baron's **jaw** dropped and his mouth opened and closed. "That won't be necessary, my boy. Couldn't you see that I was just having a joke with you?"

「我努力忍住激動的情緒，鎮定地面對著他。『我們還是會繼續準備其他的菜，我也會把那頓大餐帶去山頂，獻給神明，並且附上一張紙條跟他們解釋，美味可口的黃金覆盆子已經不見了，因為壞地主，也就是你，把它們撞翻掉進河裡去了。』

　　「壞地主嚇得目瞪口呆，嘴巴張大，又很快地闔上。『乖孩子，沒有那個必要嘛。你難道看不出來，我只是跟你開開玩笑而已？』

note [not] 名 短箋

jaw [dʒɔ] 名 下巴

'I folded my arms and said nothing while the Baron **pleaded** with me to take all the golden raspberries I needed.

'Finally, I shook my finger at him. "Oh, you will have to do much better than that. Now, Baron, say after me: Please, please most kindly, honorable and worthy Tashi, could you take the berries of this miserable worm of a Baron, who stands before you?"

'The Baron gritted his teeth and forced out the words. He even tried to smile as I picked his fruit. I thanked him politely for **holding** the basket for me.

「我雙手交叉抱在胸前，一語不發。壞地主苦苦哀求我，要我去拿所需要的黃金覆盆子。

　　「最後，我對他搖搖手指頭。『噢，這樣太便宜你了。來，地主，跟著我說：拜託，最仁慈、最尊貴、最了不起的大喜，求求你拿走這個站在你面前的可憐蟲地主的覆盆子，好嗎？』

　　「壞地主咬牙切齒，把那些話從嘴裡逼出來。當我摘覆盆子的時候，他甚至還努力要擠出笑臉來。我很有禮貌地謝謝他幫我拿籃子。

plead [plid] 動 懇求

hold [hold] 動 拿著

'It was late afternoon by the time I got back to the village and everything was ready. A wonderful omelet filled with delicate flavorsome mushrooms lay on some vine leaves upon my mother's best platter. My mouth **watered** as I lifted the lid from the dish of speckled trout in wine and ginger and **pickled** vegetables that only Big Wu and Little Wu knew how to prepare. We washed the raspberries in fresh spring water, dried them and placed them gently in a moss-lined basket.

「當我回到村子裡的時候，已經是傍晚了，一切也安排就緒了。一道美味的蛋捲由藤葉襯托著，裡頭包著香噴噴的蘑菇，擺在我媽媽最好的大盤子上。用酒和薑絲調味的斑紋鱒魚和泡菜更是只有大吳和小吳才能做得出來的拿手菜；打開這道菜的蓋子時，我的口水流個不停。我們用清涼的泉水來清洗覆盆子，晾乾以後，再輕輕把它們放進鋪有青苔的籃子裡。

water [ˋwɑtɚ] 動 流口水
pickled [ˋpɪkḷd] 形 醃製的

'Luk Ahed and I carried two baskets each and when we reached the mountain top, we spread out a gleaming white linen tablecloth and **set out** the meal. It was perfect.

'When it was nearly midnight we hid behind a tree and waited. On the stroke of twelve we were **dazzled** by a blinding silver light. We **blinked** against the light, closing our eyes for just a moment, but when we could see again the cloth was **bare**.

「盧半仙和我各提著兩個籃子，到了山頂以後，先鋪上一塊潔白的亞麻桌巾，再把大餐擺好。一切真是完美極了。

　　「快到午夜時，我們就躲在樹後面等著。十二點鐘聲一敲，忽然有一道強烈的銀色光芒，把我們照得眼花撩亂。有一陣子，銀光強烈得讓眼睛睜不開，等到我們可以睜開眼睛時，桌巾上的東西已經不見蹤影了。

set out　擺出（食物）
dazzle [ˋdæzl̩] 動 使暈眩
blink [blɪŋk] 動 眨眼睛
bare [bɛr] 形 空的

'Luk Ahed and I ran all the way back down the mountain and hurried to his house to see if my horoscope had changed. Luk Ahed peered at the chart, his **brow wrinkling** deeper with every second. I was holding my breath, and began to feel **faint**. If he didn't answer soon, I thought I might **fall over** and die right where I stood. '"Tashi, the bad news is that all our work preparing that magnificent meal was for nothing."

'"!!!???!!!??"

「盧半仙和我一路跑下山，急急忙忙地趕到他家，看看我的命盤改了沒有。盧半仙盯著我的命盤，額頭上的皺紋越擠越深。我屏住呼吸，開始覺得暈眩。我想假如他再不趕快開口說話的話，我可能就此倒地不起。

「『大喜，很不幸的，我們大家準備出來的那頓豐盛的大餐，恐怕是白忙一場了。』

「『 !!!???!!!?? 』

brow [braʊ] 名 前額

wrinkle [`rɪŋkl] 動 起皺紋

faint [fent] 形 即將昏倒的

fall over 倒下

47

'Then he smiled **guiltily**, bowing his head. "The *good* news is that you didn't need to do any of it. Look, here where I read *10th* birthday, it was really your *100th* birthday. You see, a little bit of breakfast pancake was **covering** the last zero."

'We stared at each other for a moment and began to laugh.

'"Let's not tell the village," said Luk Ahed. "They might be a little bit **cross** with me."'

「接著他低下頭愧疚地笑了笑。『幸運的是，你其實用不著那麼大費周章。瞧，這地方我原先看成是十歲生日，其實是一百歲。你看，這一小塊早餐的煎餅把最後的那個零給遮住了。』

「我們面面相覷了好一陣子，然後開始大笑。

「『咱們別告訴村人吧，』盧半仙說，『他們可能不會放過我。』」

guiltily [`gɪltɪlɪ] 副 慚愧地
cover [`kʌvɚ] 動 遮蓋住
cross [krɔs] 形 生氣的

The family looked at Tashi with their mouths
open. Uncle Joe's was still full of ghost pie,
and a **dollop** fell out onto the table.

Jack cleared his throat. 'So how do you think
you'll feel when you are nearly one hundred
and you know you're going to die?'

傑克一家人張大了嘴巴看著大喜。喬大叔的嘴裡塞滿了鬼派，有一小塊還掉到桌子上。

　　傑克清一清喉嚨。「那麼，當你快一百歲，知道自己快死了的時候，你想你心裡會有什麼感想？」

dollop [`dɑləp] 名 （食物的）團，塊

'Oh,' Tashi waved airily, 'if I'm not quite ready, I'll just prepare another perfect meal for the God of Long Life.'

'Here's to a l-o-n-g friendship then,' said Uncle Joe, raising his glass of wine. They all **clinked** glasses and **wished** each other well. Then Uncle Joe added, 'You know, Tashi, that ghost pie really was excellent. It's given me a lot of **energy**. I think I'll go and **stretch** my legs after that long meal.' And he rubbed his hands together with excitement.

「哦，」大喜不在乎地揮揮手，「要是我還不想死，我會再給長壽之神準備一頓大餐的。」

喬大叔舉起酒杯說，「這一杯，敬我們友誼長存。」他們一起乾杯，互相祝福彼此。然後喬大叔補上一句，「我說啊，大喜，那鬼派的確很棒，讓我精神百倍。一頓飯吃了那麼久，我想我也該起來伸伸腿了。」他高興地搓著手。

clink [klɪŋk] 動 發叮噹聲

wish [wɪʃ] 動 祝福

energy [ˋɛnɚdʒɪ] 名 活力

stretch [strɛtʃ] 動 伸展

'It only **lasts** for three days!' Tashi called out, but Uncle Joe had already walked through the kitchen wall, and was gone.

'Great way to travel,' he yelled from the garden. 'See you soon!' And they heard him **humming** the old song, *'No walls can keep me in, no woman can tie me down, no **jail** can hold me now, da dum da dum da dum...'*

大喜大喊，「鬼派的效用只能持續三天哦！」然而喬大叔已經穿過廚房牆壁不見了。

他在花園放聲大叫，「真是一種旅行的好方法，再見啦！」然後他們聽到他哼起那首老歌，「沒有牆壁可以把我擋住，沒有女人可以把我綁住，沒有監獄可以把我困住，答噹答噹答噹……」

last [læst] 動 持續
hum [hʌm] 動 哼唱
jail [dʒel] 名 監獄

嗨!我是大喜,

我常碰到許多有趣的事情唷!

想知道我的冒險故事嗎?

來自遠方的大喜/大喜愚弄噴火龍/大喜智取巨人/大喜與強盜

大喜妙計嚇鬼/前進白虎嶺/大喜與精靈/大喜與被擄走的小孩

大喜巧鬥巫婆/大喜妙懲壞地主/大喜勇退惡魔/大喜與奇妙鐘

大喜與大臭蟲/大喜與魔笛/大喜與寶鞋/大喜與算命仙

共 16 本,每本均附 CD

全新的大喜故事來囉！
這回大喜又將碰上什麼樣的難題呢？
讓我們趕快來瞧瞧！

Anna Fienberg & Barbara Fienberg／著
Kim Gamble／繪　　王盟雄／譯

最新
出版

大喜與寶鞋

大喜的表妹阿蓮失蹤了！
為了尋找阿蓮，
大喜穿上了飛天的寶鞋。
寶鞋究竟會帶他到哪裡去呢？

最新
出版

大喜與算命仙

大喜就要死翹翹了！？
這可不妙！
盧半仙提議的方法，
真的救得了大喜嗎？

風和日麗，天高氣爽，
可愛的小動物們又要出來搗蛋囉！
這回他們又做了什麼？！

烏龍森林

小猴子幫森林裡的動物們洗衣服，
最後卻弄得雞飛狗跳！！！？？？

鱷魚巴索

可愛的鱷魚寶寶巴索老是把他的保姆氣跑，
這個新保姆也會一樣嗎？

龍龍查理
快醒來

龍龍查理老是從年頭睡到年尾，
今兒個卻被森林裡的動物們吵醒了……

國家圖書館出版品預行編目資料

大喜與算命仙 / Anna Fienberg,Barbara Fienberg著;
Kim Gamble繪;王盟雄譯.－－初版一刷.－－臺北
市;三民,民91
　　面;公分－－(探索英文叢書.大喜說故事系列;16)
中英對照
ISBN 957-14-3622-4 　(平裝)

1.英國語言－讀本

805.18

ⓒ　大喜與算命仙

著作人　Anna Fienberg　Barbara Fienberg
繪　圖　Kim Gamble
譯　者　王盟雄
發行人　劉振強
著作財　三民書局股份有限公司
產權人　臺北市復興北路三八六號
發行所　三民書局股份有限公司
　　　　地址 / 臺北市復興北路三八六號
　　　　電話 / 二五〇〇六六〇〇
　　　　郵撥 / 〇〇〇九九九八——五號
印刷所　三民書局股份有限公司
門市部　復北店 / 臺北市復興北路三八六號
　　　　重南店 / 臺北市重慶南路一段六十一號
初版一刷　中華民國九十一年四月
編　號　S 85612
定　價　新臺幣壹佰柒拾元整
行政院新聞局登記證局版臺業字第〇二〇〇號

網路書店位址：http://www.sanmin.com.tw